What About Me?

12 Ways to Get Your Parents' Attention
(Without Hitting Your Sister)

Eileen Kennedy-Moore ❋ *Illustrated by Mits Katayama*

PARENTING PRESS
Seattle, Washington

Library of Congress Cataloging-in-Publication Data

Kennedy-Moore, Eileen.
  What about me? : twelve ways to get your parents' attention without
hitting your sister / by Eileen Kennedy-Moore ; illustrated by Mits Katayama.
     p. cm.
   ISBN 1-884734-86-3 (hardcover)
   1. Attention-seeking--Juvenile literature. 2. Child rearing--Juvenile
literature. I. Katayama, Mits. II. Title.
   BF637.A77K46 2005
   646.7--dc22
                              2005005569

Printed in China
Illustrations rendered in black ink and watercolor
Text set in Raliegh

Parenting Press, Inc.
P.O. Box 75267
Seattle, Washington 98175

www.ParentingPress.com

Dedication

To my four little angels,

Mary, Daniel, Sheila, and Brenna

— Eileen Kennedy-Moore

To my dear granddaughter Sara,

with lots of love from Bumpa

— Mits Katayama

When your parents are distracted,

And they always seem too busy,

And they just don't seem to notice you're nearby,

You could hit your little sister . . .

But you know you'd get in trouble,

So there must be something else that you could try.

You could —

Watch what they're doing and ask, "Can I help?"

Show you can do something all by yourself.

Offer to share — even give Sister half.

Make silly faces so Baby will laugh.

Draw them a picture with colors that glow.

Sing them a song in a fabulous show.

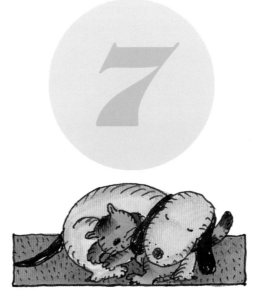

Cuddle up close for a story-time hug.

Bring them a flower, a rock, or a bug.

Show them a new trick and say, "Look at me!"

Help with the housework by cleaning with glee.

Get out some toys and invite them to play.

Tell them, "I love you" your own special way.

Busy or not, do you know what they'll do?

They'll give you a smile and say, "We love you, too!"

Note to Parents

One of the hardest things about being a sibling is having to share parents' attention. Even in the most loving home, older siblings tend to hear comments like: "Be quiet or you'll wake your sister." "We'll do that later—I have to feed the baby now." Or "Let your brother play, too." Preschoolers can't explain to their parents, "I'm feeling frustrated, jealous, and left out. I could really use some extra attention and reassurance of your love." Instead, they are likely to misbehave and even lash out by screaming, hitting, pushing, or snatching toys.

As a psychologist and a mother of four young children, I know that one of the best techniques for dealing with children's misbehavior is to teach them positive ways to ask for what they want. For example, an 18-month-old can be taught to say, "All done!" instead of dumping food on the floor at the end of a meal.

What About Me? helps children cope with feelings of jealousy or concerns about being ignored. Using a gentle and practical approach, it shows them how to express their feelings in peaceful ways, so they can get along better with their parents and siblings. *What About Me?* helps children to feel capable because it offers them choices rather than rules.

Read this book with your child several times, then leave it someplace where your child can easily use it. When your child tries a strategy in this book, be sure to react warmly with a smile, a hug, interested questions, words of praise, or a bit of one-on-one time. You may find that your home is more peaceful when your child can effectively tell you what he or she needs, and you can understand and respond in a caring way.

—*Eileen Kennedy-Moore, Ph.D.*